THE EVIL CHILDREN OF MIDWICH

Something odd has happened to the village of Midwich. It appears to be under the control of some sort of alien force. But after a few hours everything seems to have returned to normal.

Then, nine months later, a number of very strange children are born in the village. They don't look like monsters. In fact, they are extremely beautiful, but their eyes glow. And they have special powers. They can read people's minds. And they can kill just by thinking about it. . . .

Books by Daniel Cohen

BIGFOOT: *America's Number One Monster*
GHOSTLY TERRORS
THE GREATEST MONSTERS IN THE WORLD
HORROR IN THE MOVIES
THE MONSTERS OF STAR TREK
MONSTERS YOU NEVER HEARD OF
REAL GHOSTS
SCIENCE FICTION'S GREATEST MONSTERS
SUPERMONSTERS
THE WORLD'S MOST FAMOUS GHOSTS

Books by Daniel and Susan Cohen

THE KID'S GUIDE TO HOME COMPUTERS
THE KID'S GUIDE TO HOME VIDEO
ROCK VIDEO SUPERSTARS
WRESTLING SUPERSTARS
WRESTLING SUPERSTARS II

Available from ARCHWAY paperbacks

SCIENCE FICTION'S GREATEST MONSTERS

DANIEL COHEN

Illustrated with
photographs and prints

AN ARCHWAY PAPERBACK
Published by POCKET BOOKS • NEW YORK

To Ruffles

Illustrations are used by permission and through the courtesy of: Associated Film Distribution, 86; copyright © 1982, all rights reserved, The Blade Runner Partnership, 76; British Lion, 20; Columbia Pictures, 40; Library of Congress, 92; copyright © Lucasfilm (LFI 1983, all rights reserved, courtesy of Lucasfilm Limited), 53; Movie Star News, 4, 15, 23, 25, 29, 31, 37, 38, 39, 46, 51, 54, 55, 61, 62, 63, 65, 67, 72, 73, 74, 80, 81, 82, 83, 87, 94; Orion Pictures, 75; United Artists, 21; Universal Pictures, copyright © 1982, 34–35; Universal Studios, 85.

An Archway Paperback published by
POCKET BOOKS, a division of Simon & Schuster, Inc.
1230 Avenue of the Americas, New York, N.Y. 10020

Published by arrangement with Dodd, Mead & Company, Inc.
Library of Congress Catalog Card Number: 80-1017

ISBN: 0-671-44485-9

First Archway Paperback printing June, 1986

10 9 8 7 6 5 4 3 2

Printed in the U.S.A.

IL 4+

CONTENTS

1

Panic!

It began at 8 P.M. on October 30, 1938. It was the night before Halloween. All across America people were listening to the radio. Most of them were listening to Edgar Bergen and Charlie McCarthy. The ventriloquist and his wise-cracking dummy had the most popular radio show in the country.

About twelve minutes after eight, Bergen stopped telling jokes and brought on a singer. The singer was not as popular as the jokes. So many people switched stations. They heard what they thought was a live broadcast of dance music by "Ramon Raquello and his orchestra" direct from "the Meridian Room in the Hotel Park Plaza in downtown New York."

Then a very excited announcer broke in. He said that a huge object, "believed to be a meteorite, fell to Earth. It landed on a farm near Grovers Mill, New Jersey, twenty-two miles from Trenton."

A special reporter, "Carl Phillips," was being sent to broadcast live from the spot.

People forgot all about Charlie McCarthy. They wanted to find out what was happening in New Jersey.

The dance music came on once again. Then there was the voice of "Carl Phillips."

"In front of me I can see the—thing. It is half-buried in a huge pit . . . From what I can see, the object doesn't look very much like a meteor."

Phillips talked to the police and some of the people in the crowd. Then noise was heard from the crowd. Phillips said:

"Ladies and gentlemen, this is the most terrifying thing I have ever seen. Wait a minute! Someone is crawling out of the top! Someone . . . or . . . something!"

There was a cry of horror from the crowd. Phillips went on speaking. His voice was nearly hysterical.

"Good heavens, something is wriggling out of the shadows. It is like a gray snake. Now there's another one, and another. They look like huge arms to me. There, I can see the thing's body. It's as large as a bear. It is shining like wet leather. But that face. It—it's impossible to describe. I can hardly force myself to keep looking at it. The eyes are black and gleam like a snake's. The monster is rising up!"

The thing certainly didn't look friendly. And it wasn't. Phillips went on to describe how two policemen walked toward the monster, carrying a flag of truce.

"A humped shape is rising out of the pit. I can make out a small beam of light against a mirror. What's that? There's a jet of flame coming from the mirror. It is coming right at the advancing men. It strikes them head-on! Oh, no, they're turning into flame!"

Then there was a loud crash. The microphone went dead.

By this time panic had broken out among many of the radio listeners. It was worst in places near Trenton where the alien invaders were supposed to have landed. Roads were jammed with people trying to escape the invaders. Others grabbed guns and rushed off to fight them.

On the radio the situation was growing worse and worse. A man called "Captain Lansing of the state militia" said that 7,000 men were closing in on the spaceship. Then there was another long pause, and a new voice.

"Ladies and gentlemen, I have a grave announcement to make. Incredible as it may seem, these strange beings who have landed in the Jersey farmlands tonight are the first part of an invading army from the planet Mars. The

Earth people destroyed by Martian weapons, from the film *The War of the Worlds*.

battle which took place tonight at Grovers Mill has ended. It is one of the worst defeats ever suffered by an army. Seven thousand men armed with rifles and machine guns have been destroyed by a single fighting machine."

The announcer went on to say that the Martian machines were moving in the direction of New York City. He described how the things were crossing the Hudson River and spreading poison gas over the city.

People in New York City—the real New York City—rushed out of their homes to see what

The New York Times

Copyright, 1938, by The New York Times Company.

NEW YORK, MONDAY, OCTOBER 31, 1938.

Radio Listeners in Panic, Taking War Drama as Fact

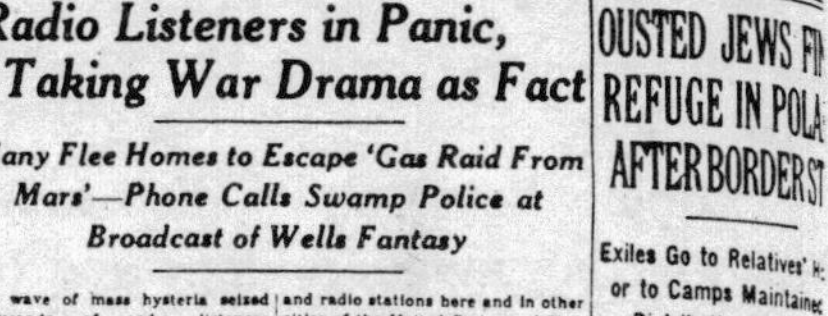

Many Flee Homes to Escape 'Gas Raid From Mars'—Phone Calls Swamp Police at Broadcast of Wells Fantasy

A wave of mass hysteria seized thousands of radio listeners throughout the nation between 8:15 and 9:30 o'clock last night when a broadcast of a dramatization of H. G. Wells's fantasy, "The War of the Worlds," led thousands to believe that an interplanetary conflict had started with invading Martians spreading wide death and destruction in New Jersey and New York.

The broadcast, which disrupted households, interrupted religious services, created traffic jams and clogged communications systems, was made by Orson Welles, who as the radio character, "The Shadow," used to give "the creeps" to countless child listeners. This time at least a score of adults required medical treatment for shock and hysteria.

In Newark, in a single block at Heddon Terrace and Hawthorne Avenue, more than twenty families rushed out of their houses with wet handkerchiefs and towels over their faces to flee from what they believed was to be a gas raid. Some began moving household furniture.

Throughout New York families left their homes, some to flee to near-by parks. Thousands of persons called the police, newspapers and radio stations here and in other cities of the United States and Canada seeking advice on protective measures against the raids.

The program was produced by Mr. Welles and the Mercury Theatre on the Air over station WABC and the Columbia Broadcasting System's coast-to-coast network from 8 to 9 o'clock.

The radio play, as presented, was to simulate a regular radio program with a "break-in" for the material of the play. The radio listeners, apparently, missed or did not listen to the introduction, which was: "The Columbia Broadcasting System and its affiliated stations present Orson Welles and the Mercury Theatre on the Air in 'The War of the Worlds' by H. G. Wells."

They also failed to associate the program with the newspaper listing of the program, announced as "Today: 8:00-9:00—Play: H. G. Wells's 'War of the Worlds'—WABC." They ignored three additional announcements made during the broadcast emphasizing its fictional nature.

Mr. Welles opened the program with a description of the series of

Continued on Page Four

MEAD STANDS PAT AS A NEW DEALER IN BID FOR SENATE

Democratic Candidate Opposes Any Except Minor Changes in Labor and Security Laws

UPHOLDS THEORY OF TVA

Wants Budget Balanced, but Not if This Means 'Misery,' He Tells The Times

Text of Representative Mead's reply is printed on Page 6.

From a Staff Correspondent

BUFFALO, N. Y., Oct. 30.—Representatives James M. Mead, Democratic candidate for the short-term Senatorial seat in the election Nov. 8, today answered in a statement the six questions on campaign issues propounded by THE NEW YORK TIMES to the four New York nominees of the two major parties in an editorial Oct. 20.

Mr. Mead's answer, in the main, was a broad and little qualified defense of the New Deal legislation which he, as a member of the House of Representatives, had a part in formulating and passing.

The principles of the Social Security and National Labor Relations Acts he defended stoutly, seeing need only for revisions to extend the benefits of the former, a correction of technical defects and a tightening of administration.

Principal opposition to the Social Security Act he saw inspired by those who fear that it will "become too important a monument to the Democratic party and to men like President Roosevelt and Senator Wagner."

Opposes "Pay-as-You-Go" Policy

He unqualifiedly opposed a revision of the law to make social se-

B. C. VLADECK DIES; CITY COUNCILMAN

American Labor Party Chief Here Was Manager of The Jewish Daily Forward

B. Charney Vladeck, American

DALADIER PREPARES TO RULE SEVERELY

Calls Cabinet Meeting to Talk Over Decrees to Promote Recovery in Industry

By P. J. PHILIP

OUSTED JEWS FI[ND] REFUGE IN POLA[ND] AFTER BORDER ST[AY]

Exiles Go to Relatives' H... or to Camps Maintained ... Distribution Committee

REVEAL CRUELTY OF ...

Others Sent Back to Germ... Pending Parleys on Issue ... the Two Governments

Wireless to THE NEW YORK TIMES.

WARSAW, Poland, Oct. ...—evacuation from frontier ... thousands of Polish Jews—... cording to official reports ... 12,000 according to an estimate ... the Jewish Relief Committee ... ported from Germany began ... after they had been massed ... frontier stations up and down ... border for twenty-six hours ... terrible ordeal is nearing its end.

Polish authorities have permitted officials of the Joint Distribution Committee to send the victims to relatives' homes in Poland ... special camps the committee maintains. The refugees spent a ... less night in barracks, crowded ... tion buildings or empty ... cars; many spent the night ... open in the no man's land between the frontiers.

The Joint Distribution Committee supplied food and will also pay ... cially reduced railway fares ... interior.

It is believed that the evacuation will last another day or so ... refugees desire to remain ... frontier area pending the ... of the Warsaw-Berlin negotiations which may result in the repeal of the deportation order, ... them to return to their homes in Germany.

Suffering Is Described

Reports from various points ...

Orson Welles's radio drama made front-page news.

was going on. Many called police stations asking for gas masks. In one building in Newark tenants actually rushed out into the street with wet towels covering their faces. They believed they had been gassed.

A woman ran into a New York theater shouting that the world was coming to an end. A man swore that he heard President Roosevelt on the radio ordering the evacuation of New York City.

People who stuck by their radios heard how the Martian invaders appeared over other cities. Then there was a pause, followed by these words:

"You are listening to the broadcast of Orson Welles and the 'Mercury Theatre on the Air.' This is an original broadcast of *The War of the Worlds* by H.G. Wells. The broadcast will continue after a short intermission."

It was not a news program at all. It was a radio play. The play was based on a famous science fiction story. People who had listened to the program from the beginning knew this. An announcement had been made at the start of the show. There had never been any attempt to fool the listeners deliberately. Orson Welles just wanted to make the show sound realistic. No one expected the reaction the show got. People believed it. They even began to hear things and see things that weren't there.

Orson Welles, who created a panic with his *War of the Worlds* radio broadcast in 1938.

If people had bothered to turn to other radio stations they would have heard the ordinary shows. Charlie McCarthy was still making his wisecracks. There were no news bulletins on other stations. If the world was being invaded by monsters from space, surely other stations would have covered the event. But people didn't think. They were too scared.

Why had *The War of the Worlds* broadcast created such a panic? That question has been asked over and over again. There were several reasons.

First, it was a good show.

Orson Welles, who produced the show, was only twenty-three years old at the time. He was known as the "boy genius" of radio broadcasting. He went on to direct and star in some of the best films ever made in America. A Welles production could be very convincing.

Second, people were already nervous about the news.

War was about to break out in Europe. Hitler's Germans were getting ready to march into Poland. In the Far East the power of Japan was expanding. People were expecting to hear bad news over the radio. Some people got confused. They thought that they heard the Germans were invading New York, not the Martians.

But the third reason is the strongest of all.

The invading Martians, as shown in an illustration from the original story, *The War of the Worlds*.

Back in 1938 people really believed that we might be invaded by monsters from outer space. We still believe it today. No, most people don't think that it is going to happen tomorrow. But they think it *could* happen.

What if Orson Welles had done a broadcast about Count Dracula landing in New Jersey? What if he had broadcast news bulletins about a werewolf killing people in New York, or the Frankenstein monster loose in Connecticut? How many people do you think would have believed such programs? Not many, no matter how well done they had been, and no matter how nervous people already were.

In the movies or on television the vampire and the werewolf may scare us. But we don't really believe they exist. We are not quite so sure about monsters from outer space.

There may be millions or billions of worlds out in space. Some of them may be inhabited. With our space program we are trying to reach other worlds. How do we know that other worlds are not trying to reach us? We don't.

And we don't know if these other-worldly creatures are friendly. They might truly be monsters like the Martians in *The War of the Worlds* story.

That is why monsters from science fiction are probably the most terrifying monsters in the world today. Science fiction is about things that *might* happen.

In this book we are going to look at some of the more famous monsters from science fiction. These are creatures that have appeared in books, movies, and on television.

They aren't real—yet.

2

Invasion

The Orson Welles pre-Halloween broadcast was based on a story written by H.G. Wells. The two last names sound the same, but the two men were not related. The names are not spelled the same. H.G. used only one "e" in his last name.

H.G. Wells was an Englishman, born in 1866. He was one of the earliest science fiction writers. He is still considered one of the best.

The story on which the broadcast was based was called *The War of the Worlds.* It was written in 1898. It may not have been the first "invasion from space" story, but it set the style for hundreds of other stories about monstrous invaders from space.

Wells's creatures from outer space were from Mars. They were monsters and looked the part:

"A big grayish rounded bulk, the size perhaps of a bear, was rising slowly and painfully out of the cylinder. As it bulged up and caught the light, it glistened like wet leather. Two large dark-colored eyes were regarding me steadfastly. The mass that framed them, the head of the thing, it was rounded and had, one might say, a face. There was a mouth under the eyes, the lipless brim of which quivered and panted, and dropped saliva. The whole creature heaved and pulsated convulsively."

The aim of these Martians was to conquer the Earth. They were more intelligent than human beings, and their weapons were more powerful. Any humans that stood in their way were killed without mercy, without thought. The Martians in the story had no more regard for human life than humans have for the lives of flies and rats.

That was one of the points that Wells was trying to make. If the humans had the power, would they behave any differently from the Martian invaders? He wrote, "And before we judge them too harshly, we must remember what ruthless and utter destruction our own species has brought, not only upon animals, but upon its own races."

Wells was also thinking of the terrible weapons that nations were developing even then. Back in 1898 he was trying to tell people that another war would be far more terrible than

Publicity shot for *The Mysterians,* a Japanese "invasion from space" film.

they imagined. When World War I broke out, it proved that H.G. Wells's predictions of the horrors of war had been all too accurate.

In the story *The War of the Worlds* the monstrous Martians seem unstoppable. Then suddenly they begin to die. They are killed by Earth germs. Human beings are immune to the germs. To the Martians they are deadly.

Aside from the famous radio play, *The War of the Worlds* was also made into a movie in 1953. Then in 1975 came a made-for-TV movie called *The Night That Panicked America.* It was all about the famous Orson Welles broadcast.

The monster and the girl were familiar figures in science fiction pulp magazines.

In 1928 the French writer, André Maurois, gave the "invasion from outer space" theme a twist. In his story the world is about to go to war. To stop the war some newspapermen plan a hoax. They say that there are aliens on the moon who are about to attack Earth. Suddenly the enemies of Earth band together. The threatened war is avoided as the people of Earth bombard the moon with deadly rays. But there is a problem. There really *are* aliens on the moon, and they strike back.

During the 1930s and 1940s most science fiction magazines were printed on a cheap, rough paper made from wood pulp. The magazines themselves were called "pulps." In order to sell, pulp magazines had to attract the reader's attention. The best attention-getter was a monster. Usually the monster had eyes on the ends of stalks, or dozens of eyes. Science fiction fans called them Bug-Eyed Monsters, or BEMs. Month after month the pulps featured pictures of BEMs, attacking a city or carrying off a pretty girl. There were hundreds of "invasion from outer space" tales in the pulps.

The idea was used too often. People got tired of it. Today most of those stories are forgotten. But there were a few interesting variations on the theme.

In 1953 a writer named William Tenn wrote a story called *The Liberation of Earth.* A group of aliens arrive. They are extremely friendly. They say that all they want to do is help protect humans from another group of aliens who are very evil. The other aliens attack, and throw out the first group. A large portion of Earth is destroyed in the process.

When this second group of aliens takes over

Cover for a science fiction pulp magazine.

Earth, they too are friendly. They say that all they want to do is protect Earth from the first group of aliens who are the real "bad guys."

Then the first group counterattacks. The war goes on back and forth until Earth is completely destroyed. Tenn was not just writing about the future, and what might happen. He was writing about what large nations today have done to smaller ones.

Sometimes the invasion from space was treated with humor. In *Martians Go Home,* Frederic Brown wrote about an invasion of little green men from Mars. They weren't like H.G. Wells's Martians. They didn't kill people. They just made awful pests of themselves. They would peek in windows, and make all sorts of rude remarks. They would hang around when they were not wanted. And there was nothing anyone could do about them.

In *Landing Party,* Eric Frank Russell wrote of a group of alien invaders who could assume human form. An advance party landed on Earth. In order to carry out their work in secret, the aliens took the appearance of a group of humans nearby. But as soon as they entered the city they were arrested. Unfortunately for the aliens, they had landed next to a nudist colony.

Monsters don't have to be big. In Robert A. Heinlein's story, *The Puppet Masters,* the invaders are amoeba-like creatures. They attach

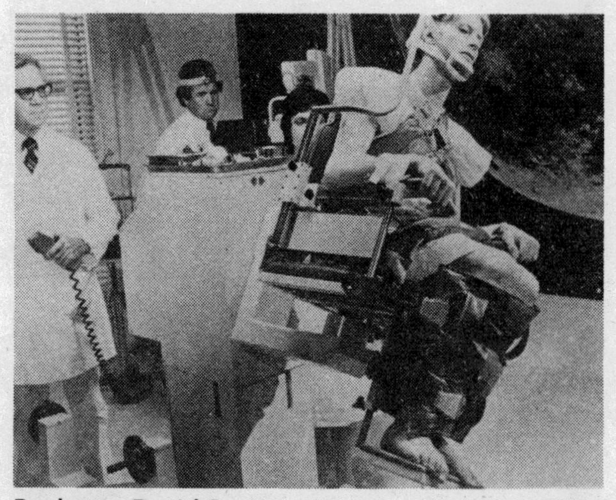

Rock star David Bowie appears as an alien in *The Man Who Fell to Earth*.

themselves to people's backs, and are able to control them.

Germs kill the invaders in *The War of the Worlds*. In Michael Crichton's novel, *The Andromeda Strain,* germs are the alien invaders. A deadly germ from space strikes a small town in America. It causes a disease that kills practically everyone who gets it. Somehow a couple of people survive the disease. Scientists try to find out how the disease from space can be stopped. But the germ is constantly changing. Finally the germ renders itself harmless.

The author of this story is a doctor. His book is filled with realistic details of medical research. It is also highly suspenseful, as the scientists rush to try and save the world. *The Andromeda Strain* was made into an excellent film in 1971.

The story *The Invasion of the Body Snatchers* was the basis for not one, but two movies. The invaders are plants. They grow giant seedpods. Exact duplicates of human beings are formed inside the pods. After the duplicates are formed, they take the place of the human beings. The pod people are planning to take over the world by replacing everyone.

A tiny plant from outer space could grow into a duplicate of a human being in *The Invasion of the Body Snatchers*. Scene is from the 1978 version of the film.

By accident, a few people discover what is happening. They try to warn others. No one will believe them. After all, the invaders don't look like monsters from another world. They look like ordinary people. That is the most terrifying part of the story. We might be invaded and not even know it. Our next-door neighbor might really be from another planet.

The original version of the film was made in 1956. It starred Kevin McCarthy and Diana Winter. Usually remakes of films are not as good as the original. But the remake of *The Invasion of the Body Snatchers*, made in 1978, was every bit as good as the original. Perhaps even better. It starred Donald Sutherland and Leonard Nimoy (better known as Mr. Spock of *Star Trek*). Kevin McCarthy from the original film had a small part in the remake.

Most of the outer space invaders in movies are more conventional monsters. There is, for example, Ymir in the 1957 film *Twenty Million Miles to Earth*. Ymir is a creature brought back by an expedition to the planet Venus. The returning expedition's rocket crashes in the Mediterranean. All of the expedition members except one have contracted a fatal disease on Venus.

They brought with them a small Venusian in a metal container. Once released from its container, the Venusian called Ymir begins to grow—and grow and grow—until it is over

Ymir is an unwilling invader from Venus in the film *Twenty Million Miles to Earth*.

twenty feet tall. Ymir looks like some kind of two-legged dinosaur.

The monster is captured and brought to the Rome zoo. It escapes after a spectacular battle with an elephant. Ymir tears up a good part of Rome before it is finally brought down in the Colosseum, by an artillery barrage.

Twenty Million Miles to Earth has a fairly familiar monster movie plot. The film is better than most because of the marvelous special effects created by Ray Harryhausen. The monster itself is a rather sympathetic character. Ymir never asked to be brought to Earth. Once on Earth, people kept locking it up or chasing it. All it wanted to do was protect itself.

The monster of *The Blob,* made in 1958, is much less sympathetic. How can you sympathize with a blob? It is a shapeless gooey mass from space. It lands outside a small town. The Blob is rather like an amoeba. It surrounds and absorbs everything in its path. The more it eats, the more it grows. The more it grows, the more it needs to eat.

After it absorbs a few people, the local residents get worried. What are they to do with it? You can't blow it up. That would just create a whole bunch of little blobs. They would all eat and grow. While they puzzle over the problem, the Blob keeps getting bigger and bigger. It winds up trying to eat an entire diner.

Finally the hero, played by Steve McQueen, suggests that the thing be frozen and dropped into the polar seas.

The movie was very popular. Even today there is a small group of monster film fans that consider *The Blob* one of the finest monster films ever made. *The Blob* was so popular that there was a sequel made. It was called, believe it or not, *Son of the Blob.*

Throughout the 1950s and '60s the Earth was invaded by an astonishing variety of monsters—at least according to the movies. The monsters ranged from brains without bodies (*Brain from Planet Arous,* 1958) and eyes without bodies (*The Crawling Eye,* 1958) to bats from Venus (*It Conquered the World,* 1956) to a

The monster in *I Married a Monster from Outer Space*.

monster that could assume human shape. (*I Married a Monster from Outer Space,* 1958). The last-named picture is not nearly as silly as the title makes it sound.

This type of monster film is no longer as popular as it once was. But this does not mean these films have been filed away and forgotten. They can be seen regularly on late night television or on TV film series like "Creature Features," which specialize in monster and horror films.

Two low-budget invaders from space films that have become cult favorites are *Strange Invaders* (1983) and the strange and wildly funny *Repo Man,* 1984. *The Adventures of Buckaroo Bonzai* (1984), a satire which suggets that the Orson Welles *War of the Worlds* broadcast was a coverup for a real invasion, didn't show in many theaters, but has been doing well as a videotape rental.

Television itself has provided us with a large number of monstrous invaders. One of the best appeared in the series called *Kolchak the Night Stalker.* The series started in 1974 and lasted only one season, much to the disappointment of horror and monster fans.

The hero was a rather seedy newspaper reporter named Kolchak, a part well played by Darren McGavin. Each week Kolchak confronted a new monster—a vampire, a werewolf, a zombie, and so forth. The monsters were rarely shown up close. McGavin thought that close-ups would make people think, "There's a guy in a rubber mask."

There weren't any close-ups in the space monster episode. There couldn't be. The thing was invisible. Something was killing humans and animals by draining their bone marrow. The invisible thing was finally tracked down in a planetarium. It was looking at the star charts. It turned out that the thing wasn't really an invader after all, it was just lost. It stopped by Earth for a bite to eat, and to look at a road map.

There were probably more monsters in the series *The Outer Limits* than in any other American TV series. The show ran for two seasons between 1963 and 1965, a total of 49 episodes. During the first season there was a new and horrible monster in every episode. That was the policy of the show. And the show did very well. In the second season the producers were changed, and the "monster of the week" was no longer required. The show lost viewers and was canceled.

The Twilight Zone was the longest-running and perhaps the best of all of TV's science fiction and horror series. It ran for 151 episodes between 1959 and 1964. The series was produced and hosted by Rod Serling. Serling wrote most of the scripts too.

Serling did not subscribe to the "monster a

week" philosophy of *The Outer Limits.* Many of *The Twilight Zone* episodes were really more fantasy than science fiction. But the show had its share of invaders from outer space.

The aliens didn't always look monstrous. In the episode "Will the Real Martian Please Stand Up?" the action centers around a group of strangers. They are sitting around a bar discussing which one of them is a Martian in disguise. In another episode entitled "The Invaders," the fine actress Agnes Moorehead plays the role of a farm woman whose isolated home has been attacked by two tiny creatures from space.

The best of the alien invader episodes was the one called "To Serve Man." A group of aliens comes to Earth. They seem friendly. In fact, they seem willing to do practically anything for people. The aliens have a book called *To Serve Man*. People think it's a book that will help the aliens meet man's needs. But no one on Earth can read it. The aliens promise a paradise for people who will go with them to the aliens' home planet. A lot of people agree to go. But one man remains skeptical. He tries to translate the book *To Serve Man*. Finally, just as people are streaming aboard the alien ships, he manages to translate the book. It's a cookbook.

These TV series are long gone. But from time to time they are rerun, often late at night. Some

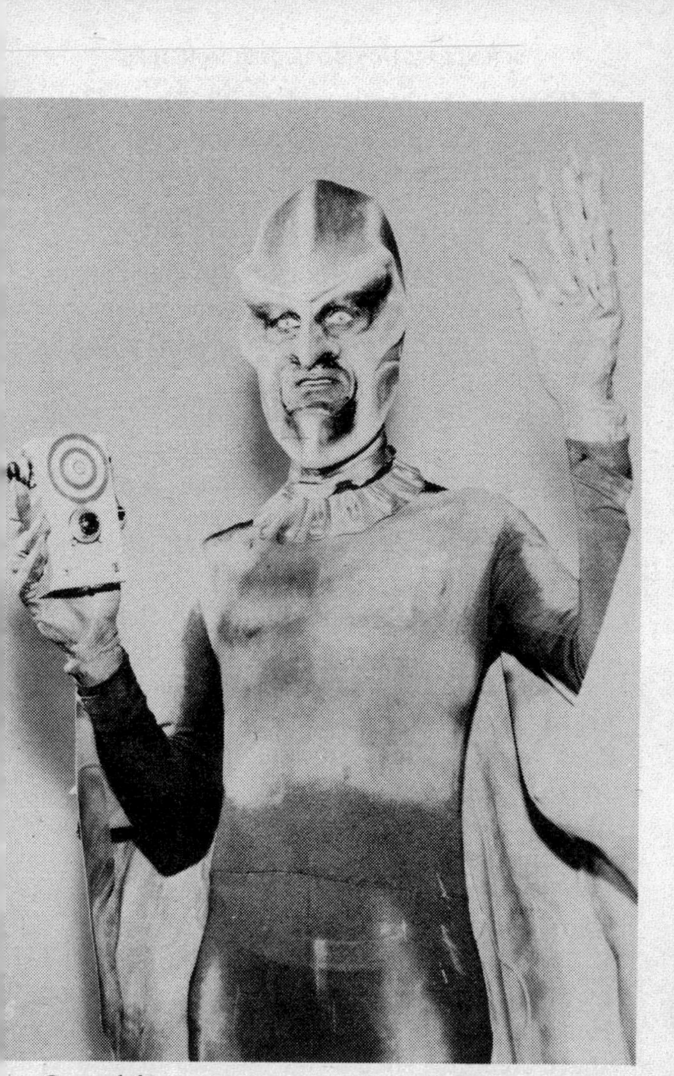

One of the many monsters from *The Outer Limits*.

of them are in black and white. The budgets were low, and the special effects poor by today's standards. But many episodes still hold up very well. If you are lucky enough to catch a good one, you can still get a scare.

Then there are the comics. In the comics, Earth was always invaded by some monster or the other. And Earth was always being saved by a superhero.

Of all of these illustrated tales, there is only one that really stands out. It is Captain Marvel's long fight against the Monster Society of Evil. The series began in *Captain Marvel Comics No. 22* and ran over 25 issues. It is a series that is considered a superclassic.

All of the monstrous villains in the world have banded together to form the Monster Society of Evil. Their leader is an unseen voice heard over a loudspeaker. The voice identifies itself as Mr. Mind. During the first few episodes, Captain Marvel defeats some of his traditional enemies like Ibac, Dr. Sivanna, and Captain Nazi. (Remember, these comics were published during World War II when Nazis were the enemy.)

Then "Cap" discovers that Mr. Mind's headquarters is on a small planetoid near the moon. Here he has to battle all sorts of monstrous space creatures such as the octopus-like Oliver. All the time "Cap" keeps searching for Mr. Mind. All he can ever find is a voice.

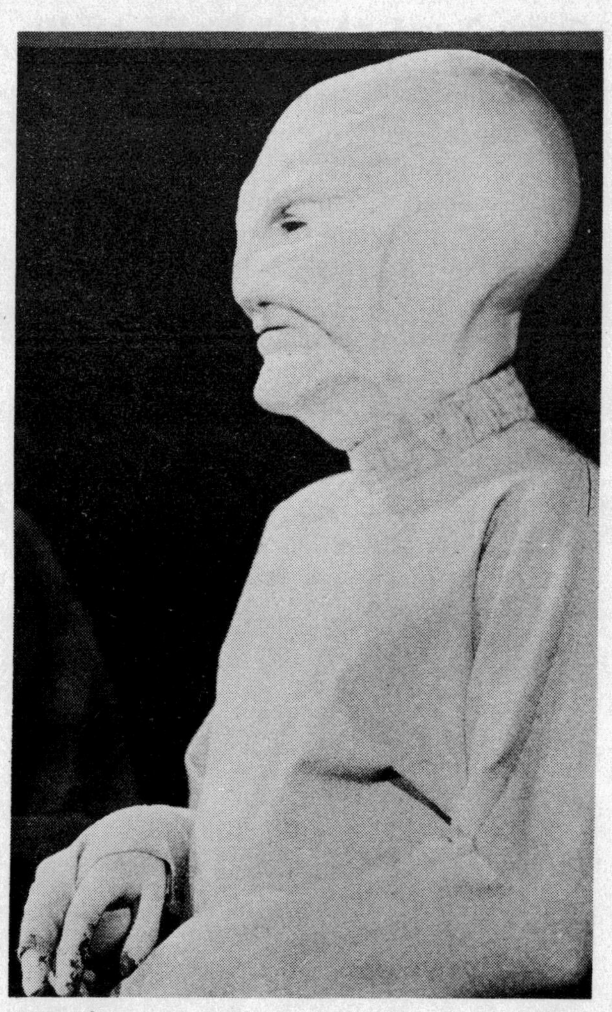

Another monster featured in *The Outer Limits*.

It wasn't until the sixth episode that Mr. Mind's shocking identity was revealed. He was a tiny worm. But he came from somewhere in space, and was very intelligent. You could tell he was intelligent because he wore glasses. Mr. Mind broadcast his thought waves through a tiny radio strung around his neck. He may have been the most unlikely looking space monster ever conceived.

Mr. Mind was small, but he was tricky. In one of the episodes he escapes by putting his glasses on an ordinary earthworm. Captain Marvel assumed the earthworm was Mr. Mind and crushed it in his hand.

The worm from space fought the World's Mightiest Mortal through a long series of adventures, before it was really killed and the world was safe at last.

3

Monsters from Flying Saucers

The modern excitement about flying saucers or Unidentified Flying Objects (UFOs) began in 1947. It was science fiction magazines like *Amazing Stories* that first gave UFOs a lot of publicity. Some science fiction fans really believed that UFOs were spaceships from other worlds. Many did not. But that didn't make any difference. Very quickly the UFO, or flying saucer, became a regular part of science fiction. For years practically every alien that came to Earth in a science fiction story landed in a round, saucer-shaped craft.

Flying saucers soon began appearing in science fiction films. One of the earliest uses of a flying saucer in a film was in *The Thing*, a 1951

In the 1982 remake of *The Thing,* the monster once again escapes from the ice.

production. Basically, it was another "invader from space" movie. But with one difference.

A ship from outer space crashes somewhere in the Arctic. It is buried under the ice. The team of scientists who go out to investigate cannot make out its shape. They spread out to form the outline of the shape. When they finish they are standing in a circle. The ship is a flying saucer. Back in 1951, when flying saucers were

on everyone's mind, the audience gasped. It was the second-best scene in the film.

The best scene was the first appearance of the monster—the Thing itself. After the crash, the monster tried to escape. But it, too, was frozen into the ice. The scientists cut out a block of ice containing the creature. They take it inside. The audience never gets a look at it.

Naturally, the monster thaws out and escapes. It begins killing people and draining their blood. The scientists search, but it always escapes them. Still, the audience never gets a clear view of it. Then, without warning, a door is thrown open, and there it is! The audience didn't just gasp, it screamed.

The Thing looked like a giant hairless human being. But it wasn't human at all. It was a vegetable. It lived on human blood. It had no more feeling about killing people than people would about eating a cabbage. The Thing, by the way, was played by the actor James Arness. He went on to become famous as Marshall Matt Dillon in the long-running TV series *Gunsmoke*.

Finally, the Thing is destroyed. At the very end of the film one of the actors warns that there are other "things" out there and we had better keep watching the skies.

The Thing was remade in 1982 into a very gory film. But despite all the graphic violence, it lacked the impact of the original. That is probably because by 1982 people didn't take flying saucers so seriously anymore.

Flying saucers in the movies did not always deliver evil creatures. In another 1951 film, *The Day the Earth Stood Still,* a giant silvery flying saucer lands in the middle of Washington. Out steps a ten-foot robot named Gort. The robot is accompanied by a very human-looking spaceman called Klaatu. They have come to warn humans to stop fooling around with atomic

Robot and flying saucer from the film *The Day the Earth Stood Still.*

weapons. If you don't, Klaatu warns, Earth will "be reduced to a burned-out cinder."

Most people simply don't believe Klaatu. So as a demonstration of his power, he stops practically every machine in the world. Then they believe him.

The film was based loosely on a story called *Farewell to the Master.* The point of the story is that the robot, not the human, is the master. This was dropped from the movie.

Gort and Klaatu were good aliens. They wanted to save the Earth. But most flying

Creatures from *Invasion of the Saucer Men.*

saucer films featured more traditional monsters. These films had titles like *Flying Disc Man from Mars* (1951), *Invasion of the Saucer Men* (1957), and *Earth vs. the Flying Saucers* (1956).

In the film *Invaders from Mars* (1953) a boy sees a flying saucer land. After that, people begin to change. They fall under the control of the Martians. The boy finally is able to convince a few adults that the world is being taken over by Martians. The Martians are green bug-eyed things with pincers instead of hands. Their leader is just a head in a transparent globe. Then it turns out that the whole thing is a bad dream.

Without a doubt, the finest of all UFO films is the 1978 hit, *Close Encounters of the Third Kind*, or *CE III*. It is considered a true classic among science fiction films. But is it just fiction? Of course, the scenes in which a giant spaceship lands near Devil's Tower in Wyoming are made up. But some of the earlier scenes are not just a filmmaker's invention. They are based on what some people claim happened to them. The film's director, Steven Spielberg, says he really believes in UFOs. Dr. J. Allen Hynek, a

Flying saucers invade London. A publicity shot for the movie *Earth vs. the Flying Saucers*.

A scene from the best of all the flying saucer movies, *Close Encounters of the Third Kind*.

scientist who also believes in UFOs, appears briefly in the film.

The creatures that step out of the UFO at the end are never shown clearly. They are roughly human in shape, but thin and stretched-out. They are also based on what people say they have actually seen.

Television took up the UFO idea. UFO episodes appeared in such series as *The Twilight Zone* and *The Outer Limits.* Batman even had a UFO episode. The Joker launches a UFO. It is, of course, a joke.

There were a few series based completely on

UFOs. A British series entitled *UFO* was shown on a few stations in the U.S. during the 1970s. The series was set in the near future. The Earth was under attack by alien spaceships. But the aliens were never seen. Nor was it ever clear what they were up to.

Project UFO was an American series. It ran for about a season and a half in the late 1970s. It was supposed to be based on real UFO cases. The main characters were two Air Force officers. They went around from place to place investigating UFO cases. Some of the cases were just sightings of alien craft. Others involved encounters with a variety of strange-looking aliens. But the series had a problem. It was not accurate enough to please UFO buffs, and not dramatic enough for ordinary TV viewers. As a result it was canceled.

The Invaders, which was first aired in 1967, was more successful. The basic idea was simple. Aliens in UFOs land on Earth. The aliens plan to take over the Earth. They have an advantage; they look just like humans. There were a few minor differences. For example, an alien could not bend his little finger.

Most people never noticed. But one man discovers what is going on. He tries to warn people. No one will believe him. They think he's crazy. To make matters worse, the aliens are out to kill him, and he can't always recognize them.

The hero of *The Invaders,* David Vincent (played by Roy Thinnes), was pursued through 43 one-hour episodes. While the aliens in *The Invaders* didn't look monstrous, they certainly tried to do terrible things to poor David.

The show was very popular for a short time. But people quickly lost interest. The episodes began to be monotonous. If you knew that David was always going to escape, there was no suspense.

Without a doubt, TV's most successful venture into the subject of UFOs was the made-for-TV movie, *The UFO Incident*. The film was shown in 1975. It was based on the book *Interrupted Journey,* which is supposed to be a true story.

It is about a couple named Betty and Barney Hill. They claimed to have been kidnapped for a short time by space creatures. When they are released they don't remember what happened to them. They can recall their "lost hours" only when hypnotized.

The aliens are shown only briefly, and never in clear close-ups. Like many of the best horror and suspense films, a good deal is left to the imagination. From what can be seen, the space creatures look small and have hairless, almost insect-like faces.

There is a lot of debate about Betty and Barney Hill's story. Some people say it is true.

Others say there is no proof, and that it is all imagination. There is no debate, however, about the fact that *The UFO Incident* is a fine, and frightening, film. If it shows on TV in your area, be sure to catch it.

4

Monsters in Space

One of the most popular films of 1979 was *Alien*. Despite the tricky special effects, magnificent sets, and wraparound sound, *Alien* is really a good old-fashioned space monster movie.

The monster is ugly. You never get a good look at it. Besides, it is always changing form and growing. But what you do see is ugly.

The monster is mean. Its whole purpose is to kill as many people as possible. No one tries to explain why it acts this way. No one tries to understand this monster, or sympathize with it.

It is the sort of monster that audiences love to hate.

There is one difference. In the end, the monster is killed by a woman. The monster had wiped out everyone else aboard the spaceship,

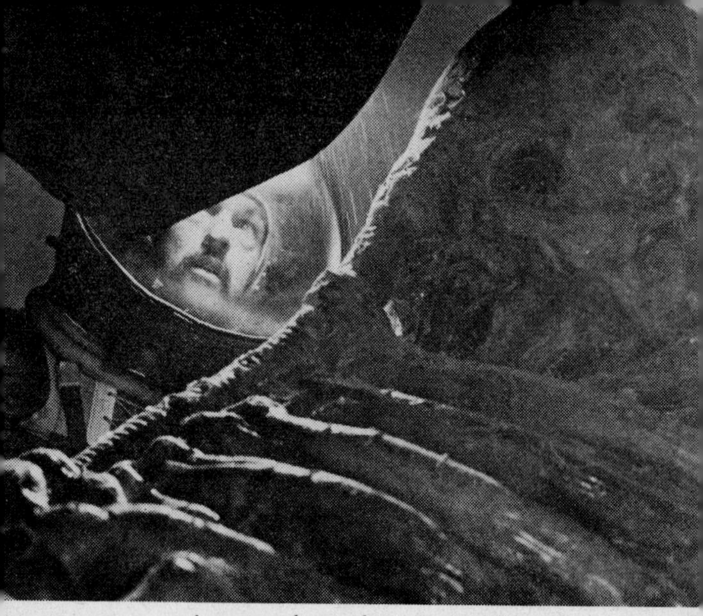

A scene from the movie *Alien*.

including the heroic captain. The last survivor is a woman (and her pet cat). She manages to shoot the thing off into space. In monster films of the past, the woman's role was usually limited to being carried off by the creature, screaming, or speaking such lines as, "Captain, I'm scared." For women, *Alien* is a breakthrough.

In science fiction not all horrible-looking creatures are supposed to be evil. In fact, Gene Roddenberry, the creator of the *Star Trek* series and *Star Trek—The Motion Picture,* doesn't even like to use the word "monster." "To be different is not necessarily to be ugly," Roddenberry has said. Horrible-looking creatures don't have to be evil. Even when they are acting in an evil way, perhaps they are just being misunderstood.

Take the Horta, for example. It appears in the *Star Trek* episode entitled "Devil in the Dark." It is a stonelike creature about seven feet long and three feet wide. It can dig through solid rock. When the crew of the U.S.S. *Enterprise* first hears of it, it has been killing off miners on the planet Janus VI. Mr. Spock and Captain Kirk track the creature down. They find out that it isn't killing for fun. The miners had mistaken its eggs for rocks. Some of the eggs had been destroyed. The Horta was just protecting itself. When everyone understands what has happened, a peaceful solution is worked out.

Then there are the Medusans. Members of this race are so hideous that no one can look at them without going mad. The only way to look at them safely is to wear special protective eyewear. At one point, Spock forgets his eyewear and looks at a Medusan. He is instantly driven out of his mind. Of course, he recovers by the end of the show.

Despite the Medusans' extreme frightfulness, they are not evil. On the contrary. They are supposed to be sensitive and to have depth of character.

The salt vampire is a more traditional monster. This creature appeared in the very first episode of *Star Trek* ever on the air. That was back in 1966. The creature had long stringy hair, a circular tooth-filled mouth, and was generally quite ugly. However, it could take on the appearance of any human being. So the viewers didn't see it in its true ugliness until the end of the show.

The salt vampire killed by sucking the salt from people's bodies. It wasn't murderous by nature. It needed the salt to survive. Still, it was not a sympathetic monster, like the Horta.

The space amoeba is sort of a giant blob. Instead of eating diners, the space amoeba eats whole star systems. When the *Enterprise* arrives on the scene, the thing is getting ready to reproduce by splitting in two. Spock manages to destroy the space amoeba by exploding an anti-matter bomb inside of it.

The *Space 1999* series was made in Britain. Its stars, Martin Landau and Barbara Bain, were Americans. From the start the series had a problem. It was always being compared to *Star Trek.* Usually *Space 1999* came off second-best in the comparison.

The basic themes were the same—a group of people wandering through space having different adventures. The producers of the *Space 1999* series insisted that it wasn't "just another *Star Trek.*" There were differences, they said. One of the differences was the monsters.

Star Trek producer Gene Roddenberry didn't like the traditional ugly, evil, space monster. The producers of *Space 1999* loved them. In the third episode there is a truly terrifying black-tentacled thing guarding a spaceship graveyard. The moment when the thing first bursts out of a hatchway is one of the best scenes in the whole series.

In the show's second season a new regular character was introduced. She was Maya, an alien woman. In her ordinary form she was very beautiful. But Maya had the ability to change herself into any life form, some quite horrifying.

Space 1999 was generally well acted, and had good special effects. When it was first shown in the U.S. it was popular. But the series never could shake the *Star Trek* comparisons. It soon turned out that many people preferred to watch *Star Trek* reruns rather than new episodes of *Space 1999*. The series was canceled at the end of its second season.

The science fiction series *Lost in Space* began in 1965 and ran for three seasons. There was a total of 83 one-hour episodes. It is still rerun from time to time, usually in the afternoon.

Lost in Space revolved around the Robinson family. They had become, as the series title said, lost in space. Practically every week they met up with a different kind of alien. Some of these creatures were quite monstrous in appearance. But the series was really aimed at young children. None of the monsters was really very frightening, no matter what they happened to look like. Everyone knew that the Robinsons would come out on top in the end anyway.

The longest-running sci-fi TV series in the world is *Dr. Who.* It is a British series that has been turning up on American TV recently. The show is about the adventures of a wacky scientist named Dr. Who. Over the years, Dr. Who has confronted, and defeated, a huge number of strange-looking aliens. The show is usually played for laughs.

Back in the days before television, kids went to movies on Saturday. There would be two films—a double feature. There would also be at least one cartoon and a serial. At the end of each serial episode the hero was in terrible trouble. It looked as if this time the villains had finally won. There seemed no way the hero could get out of it alive. The purpose of that sort of ending was to get people to come back to the movie next week and see how he got out of it. He always did get out of it somehow.

Science fiction was popular in serials during the 1930s. Two of the most popular science fiction heroes of the time came from the comics. They were Flash Gordon and Buck Rogers. Both heroes were played by Buster Crabbe in the movie serials. Of the two, Flash Gordon was

One of the many aliens from *Lost in Space*.

by far the best. Even today those serials are sometimes rerun on television.

The special effects look simple, even silly, today. The acting is not very good. Buster Crabbe was a swimming star, not an actor. But the Flash Gordon serials can still be a lot of fun. There is plenty of action and, of course, there are monsters.

Flash had to face Hawkmen, Sharkmen, Treemen, and Rockmen. He even had to wrestle a giant white ape, with a horn in the middle of its forehead, and fight off things that looked like dinosaurs.

A new Buck Rogers series began appearing on television in 1979. There are some monsters. For example, in one episode Buck battles a space vampire. But the series relies more on pretty girls than monsters.

Star Wars is the most popular science fiction film ever made. It may be the most popular film of any kind ever made. There are plenty of really weird-looking creatures in *Star Wars,* but most of them do not seem very monstrous. Chewbacca looks like an outer space version of the Abominable Snowman. Yet Chewbacca is one of the good guys.

The *Star Wars* cafe has the strangest-looking customers. Some look like insects, other like elephants. Still others look like—who knows? They may snarl and threaten, but no one is really afraid of them.

Some of the monsters from *Return of the Jedi*.

In the second of the *Star Wars* series, *The Empire Strikes Back* (1977), we meet Yoda. He is strange looking, but not really a monster. Perhaps the most monstrous things in the film are Darth Vader's giant walking tanks.

The third *Star Wars* film, *Return of the Jedi* (1983), has more monsters than any other film. There are the revolting Jabba the Hutt and all his remarkable and grotesque servants and friends. There are also some good alien life forms like the cuddly Ewoks. For a lover of movie monsters this film is pure heaven.

The 1950s and early '60s were a golden age for science fiction monster films. Some of the strangest-looking creatures appeared in the film

This Island Earth (1955). In this movie a group of aliens kidnap some Earth scientists. The aliens want the scientists to help save their home planet from destruction by a hostile neighboring planet.

It! The Terror from Beyond Space (1958) looks very much like an early, low-budget version of *Alien*. The plot is the same. And the monster comes to the same end—it is shot into space through an open hatchway. The monster looks a little different, however. The monster in *Alien* is never clearly seen, while the monster in *It* looks distinctly like a reptile. Somehow,

The monster in the film *It! The Terror from Beyond Space* is very much like the monster in the movie *Alien*.

Alien from *This Island Earth*.

when people think of monsters, they think first of reptiles.

There are any number of films in which spacemen are plunked down on "prehistoric planets" and are attacked by dinosaurs. *Voyage to the Seventh Planet* (1962) is an example of this type. The real monster of this film is a giant brain. The dinosaurs are an illusion. On the screen, however, they look more real than the brain.

Another H.G. Wells story was turned into a successful film. The movie was called *The First Men in the Moon*. It was produced in England in 1964.

The film came out a few years before humans actually did land on the moon. The space program got a lot of publicity in 1964. Moon landings were on everyone's mind.

The movie opens with a very realistic shot of a moon landing. The astronauts think they are the first men on the moon. Then they discover an old British flag, and a name attached to a rock. Someone has been on the moon before them!

They send this information back to Earth. Space program workers on Earth trace the name. They discover an old man named Bedford. He is a patient in a British nursing home. For years he has been telling people he went to the moon. No one believed him. Now they do.

The film then takes up Bedford's tale. In 1899, Bedford and his fiancée were taken to the moon by a scientist named Cavor. Cavor had discovered an anti-gravity substance. He called it Cavorite.

Using Cavorite, he built a round space vehicle. Inside it the three were carried to the moon. In the Wells tale, and the film, the moon is not the dead world we now know it to be. There are living things on the moon. The three are attacked by a gigantic lunar centipede. They are saved by the Selenites.

The Selenites are an insect-like race that lives beneath the moon's surface. Cavor decides he wants to stay on the moon. Bedford and Kate want to return to Earth. Cavor helps them. On their return to Earth, the sphere crashes into the ocean and sinks. The two escape, but without the sphere, they have no proof they have ever been to the moon.

The scene then switches back to the present. The astronauts on the moon are entering underground tunnels. This is where the Selenites lived. But there is no sign of life. All the Selenites have died off. They were killed by germs brought by the Earthmen.

Bedford then remembers that Cavor "had such a terrible cold."

Writers have more freedom in creating creatures from other worlds than do filmmakers. The writer only has to describe the creature.

He does not have to show it and make it move. Practically every imaginable kind of an alien has been described at one time or another in science fiction stories.

One of the most imaginative creators of strange creatures was Stanley G. Weinbaum. He began writing in the 1930s.

Among Weinbaum's creations were the terrifying Doughpots. These were huge masses of mindless living material. They went crashing through the jungles of Venus eating everything in their path. The Doughpots were the inspiration for all the blobs and giant amoebas of later writers.

Robert A. Heinlein created an eight-legged, metal-eating monster. In one scene it eats a second-hand Buick. Then there are Frederic Brown's Widgey Birds. These are creatures so stupid and so powerful that they fly into the ground. And they keep right on flying.

5

Monsters of Change

What will the world be like in the distant future? Will human beings still be around? If they are, will they be the same? Will the human race be replaced by something better, or worse?

Many science fiction writers have tried to answer such questions. Once again it was H.G. Wells who provided some of the earliest and most interesting answers. Wells wrote a story called *The Time Machine* in 1895. It is about a man who can travel through time. He travels far into the future. He lands in a time when the human race has evolved into two different races. They are called the Eloi and the Morlocks.

The Eloi are the more attractive race. They live on the surface of the Earth. But they are very childlike. The remains of a great civilization are crumbling around them. They no longer understand how to use the machines built by their ancestors. They live entirely on fruit grown in orchards planted centuries earlier. These orchards seem capable of endlessly renewing themselves.

Underground live the Morlocks. They look like monsters, and act like them as well. At night they prey on the helpless Eloi.

Wells saw the Eloi as the distant descendants of the masters. They were people who had machines or other people to do everything for them. In the end they could do nothing for themselves. They didn't know how to do anything for themselves.

The Morlocks were the descendants of the people who ran the machines. They had lost all traces of humanity.

In 1960 *The Time Machine* was made into a first-rate film. The Morlocks were hairy, shambling, and evil—real monsters.

The time machine turned up in a more recent science fiction film. It was called *Time After Time* (1979). The story was not written by H.G. Wells. But Wells is supposed to be the hero of the film. In *Time After Time,* Wells doesn't just write about a time machine, he invents one. He uses it to chase the killer, Jack the Ripper, into modern San Francisco. The Ripper is a monster of sorts.

Stories by the science fiction writer John

The classic pose: monster and pretty girl from the film *The Time Machine*.

From science fiction writer to science fiction hero. The British actor Malcolm McDowell plays H.G. Wells in the film *Time After Time.*

Wyndham served as the basis for two of the best sci-fi films of the 1960s. The first one was *The Day of the Triffids.*

In the story the Earth passes through a radiation cloud. Most of the people on Earth are blinded by the radiation. If that isn't bad enough, the radiation has also changed the triffids. The triffids are large plants. They had been grown for human use. But after receiving a dose of radiation, they got the ability to move. They became extremely dangerous, particularly to the blind humans. Triffids can kill people with their whiplike vines.

In the end the triffids are defeated. There will be a new generation of humans born. Though their parents may have been blind, the children will not be. The human race is saved once again.

The title of another Wyndham novel, *The Midwich Cuckoos*, was changed for the movie. The film was called *Village of the Damned*, and was released in 1960.

As the film starts, something very strange has happened to the small English village of

Walking plants were the monsters in *The Day of the Triffids*.

Midwich. It appears to be under the control of some sort of alien force. After a few hours the force leaves the village. Everything seems to have returned to normal.

Then, nine months later, a number of children are born in the village. They are very strange children. They don't look like monsters. In fact, they are extremely beautiful. But they are strange and their eyes glow. They are also exceptionally intelligent. And they have other powers. They can read people's minds, and kill just by thinking about it.

A few people realize that these children are really aliens. When they grow up, they will take over the world. They must be destroyed before they become too powerful. It isn't easy. Being able to read people's minds, the children can tell when others are plotting against them. Finally, one man manages to block his thoughts long enough to plant a bomb and blow them up.

The film was very popular. So the strange, glowing-eyed children were brought back for a sequel. It was called *Children of the Damned* (1964). This time they were not evil. They had been sent to save humanity.

During the 1950s atomic bombs were being tested by the United States and the Soviet Union. People were afraid of the tests. They knew that radiation was being released. They also knew that radiation could cause mutations—that is, changes—in living things. This

The beast destroys the roller coaster at Coney Island in the climax of the film *The Beast from Twenty Thousand Fathoms*.

fear was used in a number of movies. There was, for example, *Them* (1954). The monsters, "Them," were gigantic ants. Their growth had been caused by atomic radiation. *Tarantula* (1954) featured—in case you can't guess—a giant spider. The 1950s saw a whole series of giant insect pictures.

There are other ways in which atomic energy could affect monsters in the films. It could wake them up. That's what it did in the movie *The Beast from Twenty Thousand Fathoms.* The film was based on a story by the science fiction writer Ray Bradbury. It was made on a low budget and became the surprise hit of 1953.

The film starts with atomic tests being conducted in the Arctic Ocean. The heat of the explosion releases a dinosaur that has been trapped in the ice for millions of years. The monster slithers into the ocean, and makes its way toward New York. Along the way it sinks ships and pulls down lighthouses.

When the dinosaur reaches New York it marches through the downtown area, crushing cars and eating policemen. The army is called in. They fire heavy artillery at the beast and wound it in the neck. Then there is a new menace. The monster is bleeding. Its blood carries some kind of disease. People all around start dropping like flies.

Scientists now know that they will have to kill the thing without artillery. They finally decide to shoot it full of radioactive material.

The final fight comes in the Coney Island amusement park. The creature is wrecking the roller coaster. Those who are out to get it must climb to the top of the roller coaster to get a good shot. The beast is hit, but the wounded monster is able to finish its destruction of the roller coaster before it finally dies.

In *It Came from Beneath the Sea* (1955) the

A giant octopus attacks San Francisco in *It Came from Beneath the Sea.*

monster is a giant octopus. The octopus had not been sleeping. It had been living there deep in the ocean, not bothering anyone on the surface. Then atomic testing in the Pacific Ocean killed off much of the giant octopus' food supply. This forced it to come to the surface to look for other food. The creature seemed to have a special taste for people. After sinking a few ships it heads right for San Francisco.

The monster rips down the Golden Gate Bridge and does a lot of other damage before it is finally killed. This killing is accomplished by firing an electric torpedo into its brain.

The plots for these two films were not particularly original. But the special effects were excellent. If you see these films today, the monsters may look mechanical and phony. That is only because the techniques of making this kind of film have become much better. At the time, the monsters looked very real.

A radiation experiment gone wrong created one of today's most popular monsters, the Hulk. The Hulk is, of course, mild-mannered Dr. Bruce Banner, once he loses his temper. Dr. Banner has received an excess dose of gamma radiation. Every time he gets mad he turns into a huge, well-muscled, green-skinned creature called the Hulk.

Dr. Banner and the Hulk are no Dr. Jekyll and Mr. Hyde combination. The Hulk is not evil. He is just powerful, and kind of mindless. But somehow everything he does turns out for the best. The Hulk has become a hero, not only in the comics where he started, but on television as well. The Hulk series is one of the more successful attempts to bring a comic book superhero to television.

The Hulk had a sort of predecessor in the comics. During World War II there was a popular comic book character called the Heap. The creature appeared in *Air Fighter Comics.* The Heap had once been a German World War I flying ace named Baron Emmelman.

During World War I, Baron Emmelman was

shot down over the swamps of Poland. Somehow he managed to drag himself out of the wreckage and into the swamp. There he lay, almost dead, but not quite. He had a fantastic will to live. Slowly he was transformed by the slimy vegetation growing around him. Over the years he became a mass of human decay and swamp vegetation.

But the mass could move. And it could think, though only very dimly.

Like most monsters, the Heap was very strong and nearly impossible to kill.

The Heap may have started in the artist's mind as an evil monster. But as often happens, the monster became a hero. The creature returned over and over again, for ever more fantastic adventures. This shapeless, swampy mass became more popular than Skywolf and Airboy, the pair of heroes who were supposed to be the stars of the comic.

6

Robots, Androids, and Other Machines

Not all the monsters of science fiction are alive. Some of the best (or worst) of them are machines.

Robots are one science fiction idea that did *not* start with H.G. Wells. The idea of a mechanical man of some sort is a very old one. Even the ancient Greeks had a legend about a man made of bronze. His name was Talos. He was supposed to guard the island of Rhodes.

The word "robot" itself comes from the play entitled *R.U.R.* The R.U.R. stands for Rossum's Universal Robots. The play was written in 1921 by the Czech writer Karel Capek. In Czech, "robot" means "worker" or "forced labor."

Talos, a giant mechanical man from Greek mythology, as seen in the film *Jason and the Argonauts*.

The robots were supposed to have been created chemically by Dr. Rossum. They acted in a very mechanical way, but they looked completely human. When the play was performed, the robots were played by actors without any special makeup. At the end of the play the robots revolt against their human masters.

Today we would call Capek's robots "androids." Androids are artificial beings that look like living things. In modern science fiction, robots always look like machines even if they don't behave like machines. Androids often are passed off as human beings.

The first android to appear in a movie was in the 1926 film, *Metropolis.* The villain creates an exact mechanical duplicate of the heroine. The android then nearly leads the entire city to destruction before her true nature is discovered. The villain in this early film is halfway between mad scientist and evil magician.

Androids have been used in a number of other science fiction films. In *Alien* an android is one of the crew. None of the humans on the

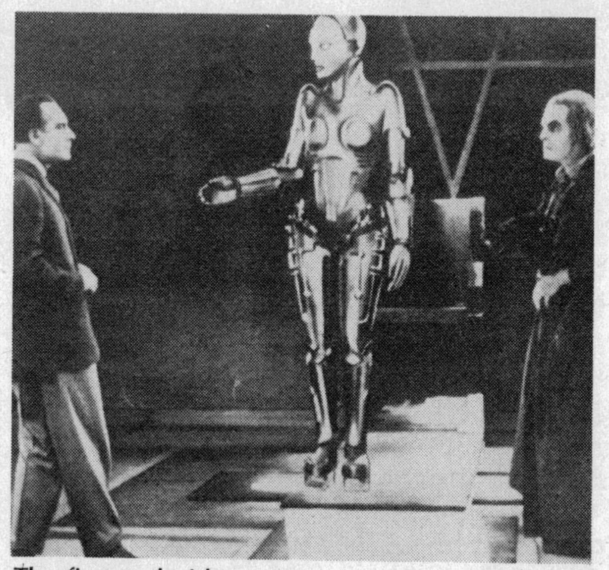

The first android to appear in a movie was in the 1926 German film *Metropolis*.

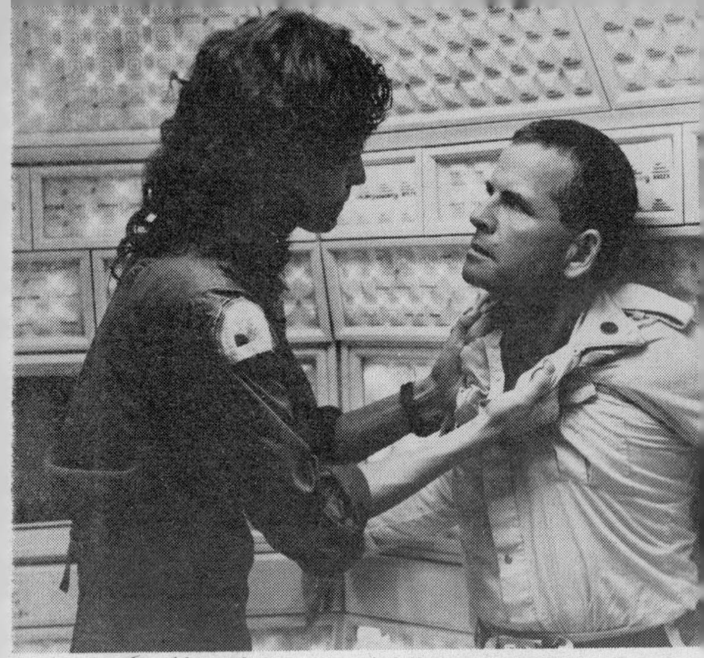

In the film *Alien,* one of the crew members turns out to be an android with an evil mission.

ship know this until it is too late. This android has been programmed to bring back the murderous alien, even if everyone is killed in the process. That is very nearly what happens. The revelation that a member of the crew is an android is one of the high points of the film.

At least the android in *Alien* was doing its job. In *Westworld* (1969) the androids are not working properly. That is why they have become dangerous. The setting is an amusement park of the future. It is a place where people can live out their dreams in different settings.

Arnold Schwarzenegger in *The Terminator*.

One of the settings is the Old West. For a price, a man can act like a cowboy. He can even gun someone down in a shoot-out. The "person" he kills is just a very realistic-looking android. A man can feel like a gunslinger without hurting anyone.

Then something goes wrong with the androids. Instead of losing all the fights, they begin winning. Because they are much stronger and quicker than humans, they soon kill off practically all the humans in the park.

In the end, one human triumphs. But this is not before being relentlessly pursued by a very

Two of the replicants from *Blade Runner*.

sinister and persistent gunfighter android played by Yul Brynner.

The film was highly successful. As with many popular films, *Westworld* was followed by a less successful sequel. It was called *Futureworld*.

Bodybuilder Arnold Schwarzenegger plays a cyborg, a flesh-covered robot, in *The Terminator* (1984). It is basically the old story of girl pursued by remorseless and nearly immortal monster, but it is very well done.

The androids (or as they are called in the film, replicants) of *Blade Runner* (1982) are complex characters. On the one hand, they are remorselessly evil. On the other, they are highly sympathetic. *Blade Runner* is one of the finest science fiction films ever made. If you have not yet seen it, you should. It is widely available on videocassette.

There was an attempt to make an android the star of a television series. After the *Star Trek* series was canceled, producer Gene Roddenberry tried to sell several other science fiction series ideas. One of them was about an android. The pilot episode was shown in 1974 as a TV movie called *The Questor Tapes.* In the show the android (played by Robert Foxworth) managed to get out of the laboratory in which it was created. Roddenberry fans waited for further adventures of the android. But the series was never produced.

Androids, good and bad, figured prominently

in the *Star Trek* series. In one episode a brilliant scientist named Dr. Roger Korby has replaced his own injured body with an android body. He plans to take over the galaxy by replacing important people with androids under his control. He even makes an android duplicate of Captain Kirk. Mr. Spock soon sees through that scheme.

Originally Korby was a good man. But when he took an android body he lost many of his basic human feelings. This made him evil. When he finally realizes what has happened, he kills himself.

The episode also featured a giant hairless android called Ruk. The part was played by a huge actor, the late Ted Cassidy. Cassidy was best known as the butler, Lurch, in the comic series, *The Addams Family.*

The *Star Trek* episode called "Mudd's Planet" was about good androids. They were too good. They had been programmed to serve humans. But the race that had built them died off. They had nothing to do. When the androids get the crew of the *Enterprise* in their grip, they practically kill them with kindness.

Androids of one sort or another also appeared in episodes of such series as *Voyage to the Bottom of the Sea, The Outer Limits, The Twilight Zone,* and *The Avengers.* The best-known android character on television was Hymie the robot. He was called a robot but he was completely lifelike. Hymie popped up regularly on the comic mystery series *Get Smart*.

The producer of *Get Smart* tried to promote a Hymie-like character as the co-star of a series. The series was called *Holmes and Yo-Yo*. It was about two cops. One of the cops, Yo-Yo, was a very lifelike robot. The series was on the air briefly in 1976, but failed to attract an audience and was canceled.

The monster robot was a popular feature of early science fiction. It was usually a huge, mindless, metal creature. The robot was completely under the control of an evil scientist. Often it turned on its creator at the end of the tale. It was a mechanical zombie—dangerous, but not very interesting.

A young science fiction writer by the name of Isaac Asimov became fed up with the monster robot idea. He wanted to write about robots that were sympathetic. If people made robots, he reasoned, they would be made to serve, not destroy. So in December, 1940, Asimov came up with what are known as the three laws of robotics.

1. A robot may not injure a human being or, through inaction, allow a human being to come to harm.
2. A robot must obey the orders given it by human beings, except where such orders would conflict with the first law.
3. A robot must protect its own existence as

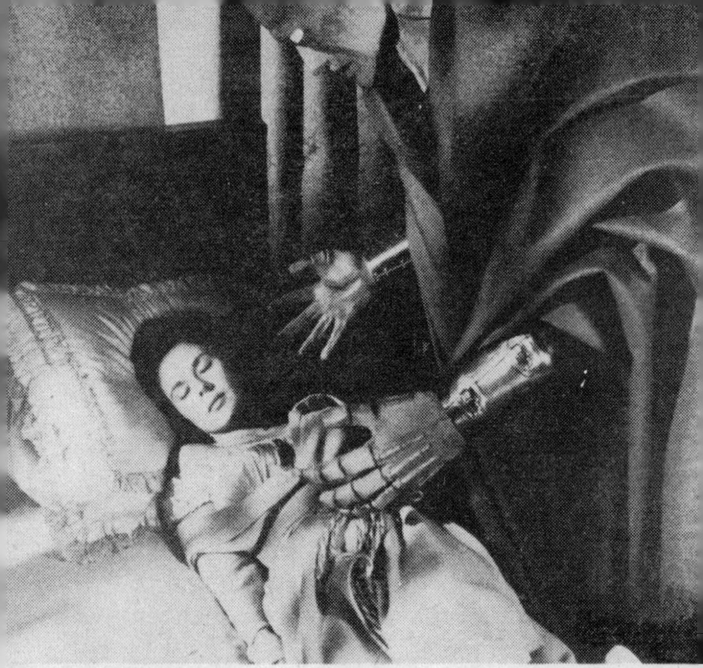

Once again the monster—in this case a robot—prepares to carry off the girl. This is in the film *The Colossus of New York*.

long as such protection does not conflict with the first or second laws.

Asimov has used the laws of robotics in many of his stories. Other science fiction writers have used them as well. Most of these stories show that the perfect robot might not be such a good idea after all.

In a story by Jack Williamson called *With Folded Hands*, we meet robots who are to "serve and obey, and guard men from harm." This creates big problems. A person could be harmed driving, or shaving, or crossing the street. Robots must protect people every moment. Humans are not allowed to do anything for themselves. In the end it is the robots who become the masters.

For many years the robots in films did not obey the laws of robotics. They were pretty evil. During the 1950s, movies like *The Mysterians*, *Kronos*, *Gog*, and *The Colossus of New York* featured giant robots. They acted like most other film monsters of the time. They killed people and destroyed whole cities. Robots were

A very machine-like and evil robot from the film *Gog*.

the servants of alien invaders in the films *Earth vs. the Flying Saucers* (1956) and *The Man from Planet X* (1951).

In 1956, a robot star was born. He was Robby the Robot. Robby appeared in the popular film

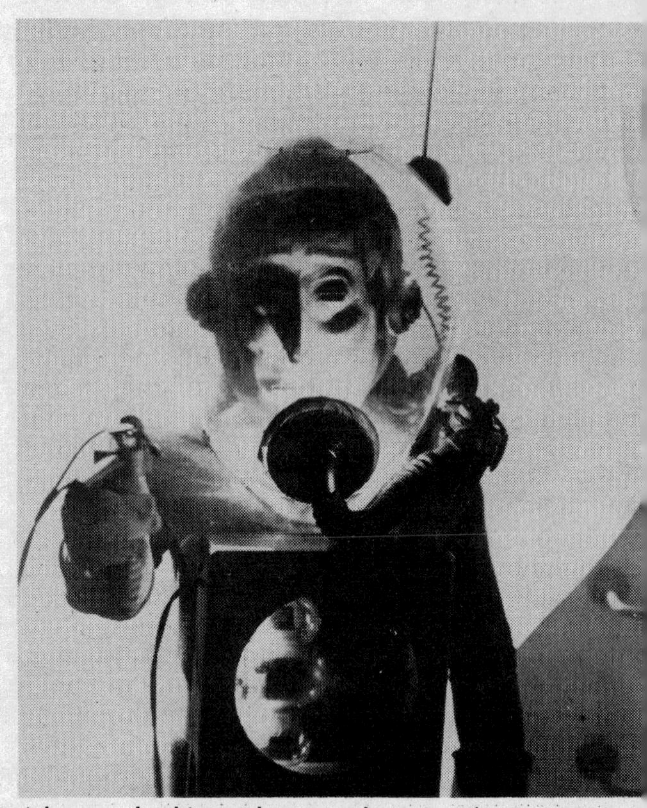

A human-looking robot was the scout for an invasion in *The Man from Planet X*.

Robby the Robot was the hero of *Forbidden Planet,* and the first in a long line of "cute" robots.

Forbidden Planet. There was a monster in the film, but it wasn't Robby. Robby was a friendly robot. He was more than friendly. He was smart, brave, and very funny. In fact, Robby stole the show.

At about the same time a friendly, funny, and smart robot became the most popular character of the *Lost in Space* series. This robot started out as sort of a villain. It began receiving so much fan mail that the producers changed it to a hero.

Then came R2D2 and C3P0, the unquestioned stars of *Star Wars*. The Walt Disney Studios' science fiction film, *The Black Hole*, also features "cute" robots, but there are evil ones as well. In the new Buck Rogers TV series, Buck's sidekicks are a couple of "cute" robots.

The old evil robot has not disappeared completely. The most persistent villains of the British *Dr. Who* series are the robot Daleks. The Daleks are really living brains in metal bodies. Long ago the Daleks lost their own bodies. They had to replace them with machinery. Perhaps because of that loss, the Daleks seem to hate everything. But their plans to conquer the universe are always foiled by Dr. Who.

The TV series and feature film *Battlestar Galactica* has robot villains. They are called Cylons. A giant robot known as Hector is the menace in the 1980 film, *Saturn 3*. Hector is

Leader of the Cylons in the film and TV series *Battlestar Galactica*.

unusual looking. He has an extra hand where his head should be.

Other sorts of machines can become villains. Take, for example, Nomad. Nomad appeared in one of the *Star Trek* episodes. It was an early space probe that had been damaged by a meteor. Later it had combined with an alien space probe. The result was a mad and murderous machine that very nearly destroyed the crew of the *Enterprise*.

The same idea was used in a spectacular way in *Star Trek—The Motion Picture*. This time the broken machine was an early Voyager probe. It

Hector, a giant robot gone mad, in the film *Saturn 3*.

had been damaged, and then fixed by alien machines. The alien machines had given it the power to destroy the whole solar system. But it wasn't truly evil. It was just confused.

One of the most popular villains in science fiction is the giant computer—the electronic "brain" that somehow gains control of those who created it.

This theme has been used countless times in science fiction stories. It has also been used on television and in the movies.

Many science fiction fans still consider *2001: A Space Odyssey* (1968) the finest science fiction movie ever made. The most memorable character in the film is a computer called HAL. HAL controls the spaceship that is taking astronauts to Jupiter. But something goes wrong with HAL. It destroys all the astronauts except one.

Perhaps the ultimate computer story was

In the film *2001: A Space Odyssey,* HAL the computer controls a spaceship bound for Jupiter. But HAL malfunctions and kills all aboard except one.

written by Frederic Brown. It is called *Answer.* In the story all of the computers in 96 billion inhabited worlds are linked together. They are linked up so that they can give the answer to the ultimate question: "Does God exist?"

The computer replies, "He does now."

7

What Was It?

Must all the creatures in the universe have bodies like we do? Why should they? Some creatures could be invisible to us. Some could have bodies made up of pure energy.

Ideas such as these have often been used by science fiction writers. They were used even before there was such a thing as science fiction. What may be the first story about an invisible monster was written back in the middle of the last century by an Irish-American writer named Fitz-James O'Brien. The story is called *What Was It?* It is about a man who is sleeping in his bed one night when he is suddenly attacked by something he can feel but cannot see. He wrestles with the thing and finally manages to tie it up.

Later he knocks the thing out with chloroform and makes a clay cast of the invisible body. It is shaped like a man. It is about four feet tall, and very muscular. The face was the most horrible thing he had ever seen. "It looked as if it was capable of feeding on human flesh."

The author does not try to explain where the thing came from. He just leaves you with the creepy feeling that there might be more of them out there.

Another nineteenth-century writer who used an invisible monster was Guy de Maupassant. De Maupassant was a French writer who died in 1893. In the years before his death de Maupassant began to go insane. The more his brain became affected, the weirder his stories became. His invisible monster story, called *The Horla,* was one of the last he ever wrote.

A man begins to think there is some invisible thing following him. He does not know what it is. His energy seems to be draining away. The thing begins to take control of his will.

Slowly he comes to realize that the invisible thing is called the Horla. It lives on human beings. Just as we enslave and eat animals, the Horla enslaves and eats people. It is the next step in evolution.

"A new being? Why not? It was assuredly bound to come! Why should we be the last?"

The man tries to kill the Horla by burning

down his own house. But he fails. The story ends with these words:

"No-no-without any doubt—he is not dead—Then-then-I suppose I must kill myself . . ."

Was the Horla really supposed to exist, or was the whole thing a product of the man's imagination? The reader has to make up his or her own mind about that.

The American writer Ambrose Bierce also wrote about an invisible monster. The story is called *The Damned Thing.* It is about a hunter whose friend is attacked and killed by an invisible monster. No one believes the hunter. They think the friend was killed by a mountain lion, and that the hunter is crazy.

The hunter says, "The human eye is an imperfect instrument . . . I am not mad; there are colors that we cannot see.

"And, God help me! The Damned Thing is of such a color."

O'Brien, de Maupassant, and Bierce are not usually thought of as writers of science fiction. But there are plenty of science fiction writers who did write about invisibility. As usual, the most famous story was written by H.G. Wells. The story is *The Invisible Man*. It is about a scientist who discovers a formula for making himself invisible.

Stories about invisible creatures have rarely

Writer Ambrose Bierce created an invisible monster in his story *The Damned Thing*.

been made into films. There is a simple reason for this. Films show things. With an invisible creature, there is nothing to show. The exception is *The Invisible Man*. That was made into a movie by Universal Studios in 1933. Universal was the same studio that made the horror classics *Dracula, Frankenstein,* and *The Wolf Man*. *The Invisible Man* ranks right up there with them.

There is one interesting sidelight about the film. The invisible man part was first offered to Boris Karloff. Karloff turned it down. For nearly the entire picture the invisible man is not seen, or is seen only wrapped in bandages. He only becomes fully visible for a moment at the end. Karloff didn't want to star in a film in which he was barely seen. So the part was offered to an unknown British actor named Claude Rains. Rains grabbed it. Invisible or not, the film made his career. Vincent Price took over the part in the sequel, *The Invisible Man Returns* (1940). Being invisible didn't hurt his career either.

A series based on the invisible scientist idea was popular on British television. In the *Invisible Man* film the scientist is evil. On television he was the good guy. An American version of the British show was made in 1975. It was not successful, and did not even last a full season.

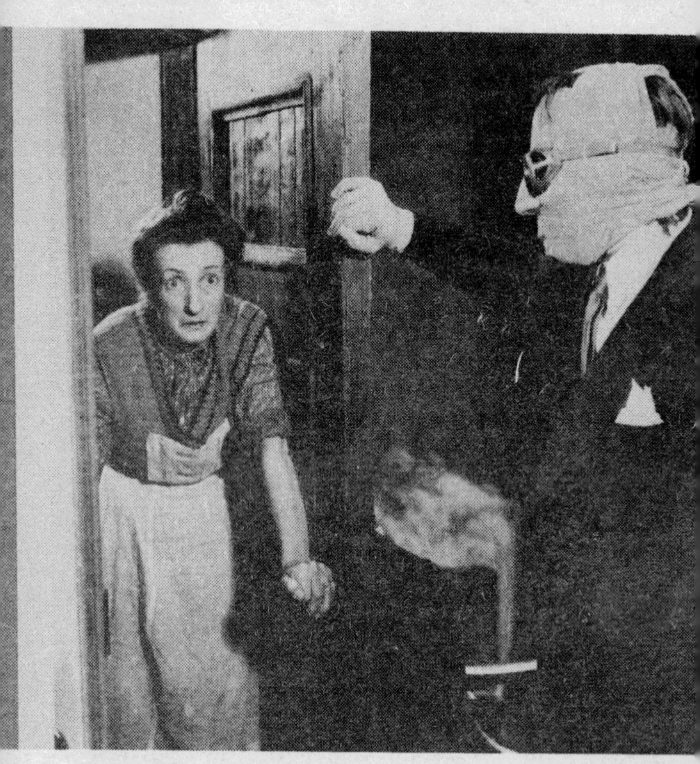

Scene from the film *The Invisible Man*. Under the bandages, suit, and gloves, there was nothing.

You might argue that the invisible man, even the evil one, is not truly a monster. But there was a real, undisputed, invisible monster in the 1956 film *Forbidden Planet*.

As the movie begins, a United Planets spaceship is nearing the planet Altair IV. The mission is to find out what happened to the colony that was started three years ago.

When the ship arrives, the crew discovers that all the colonists have been killed by some invisible force. The only survivors are Dr. Morbius and his daughter. Why were they spared when everyone else was killed? No one knows.

Altair IV had once been inhabited by a highly developed race called the Krell. They had died off long before the humans arrived. But their powerful machinery was still in working order beneath the planet's surface.

Soon the same invisible force begins attacking the crew of the spaceship. Once again Dr. Morbius and his daughter seem immune. Finally, it is discovered that the "invisible monster" is really the evil side of Morbius's own unconscious mind. His feelings and hatreds were made real by the machines of the long-dead Krell. Even Morbius did not know what was going on. When he realizes he is responsible, he throws himself to the invisible monster and is destroyed. At the same time the monster is also destroyed.

Near the end of the film, before Morbius's death, the invisible monster steps into an electrical field. At that moment it can be seen, though only in outline. It looks like a flesh-eating dinosaur.

The most evil creature in all the *Star Trek* adventures is also invisible. It is an energy creature called Red Jack. No one knows where Red Jack came from. It seems to be immortal, and it feeds on the emotion of fear. In order to eat, it creates fear.

Red Jack has appeared at various times throughout history. Its first known appearance was in London in 1888. There it was responsible for the deaths of several women. The crimes were attributed to an unknown killer called Jack the Ripper. It is from this that the name "Red Jack" was taken. At other times and places Red Jack was responsible for other unsolved murders.

The creature kills a dancer on the planet Argelius II. As it happens, the *Enterprise* crew was on the planet at the time of the killing. Chief Engineer Scott, who had been with the dancer, is accused of the crime. Scotty can't remember a thing.

Kirk doesn't believe that Scotty can be a killer. He gets Red Jack aboard the *Enterprise*. There Dr. McCoy gives everyone in the ship massive doses of tranquilizers. They don't fear anything. With no fear to feed on, Red Jack begins to starve. Finally, the thing is captured and beamed off into space.

In another episode there is a very similar creature called the Entity. Like Red Jack, it also feeds on emotions, fear and hate. In order to feed, the Entity provokes fights and wars. It causes a fight to break out between the crew of the *Enterprise* and their old rivals, the Klingons.

The cool Mr. Spock sees what is happening. He manages to convince both the Klingons and his fellow crewmembers to stop fighting. They drive the Entity out by laughing at it. It can't stand laughter.

The Entity is not entirely invisible. It appears as a cloud of rotating lights. Red Jack appears only as a computer picture. It is like a red mist.

What is the most frightening of all of the monsters of science fiction? I suppose everybody has his or her own favorite. And I have mine. Like the other creatures discussed in this chapter, my favorite does not have a solid body. It appears only as a color.

The thing—it has no name—is in a story called *The Colour Out of Space*. The story was written in 1927 by H.P. Lovecraft. Lovecraft is not usually thought of as a writer of science fiction. He is better known as a writer of horror stories. He is probably the second-best American writer of horror stories. The best in America, and the world, was Edgar Allan Poe.

In the story, a meteor lands near a remote New England farm. Scientists come to examine it. It is not like anything they have ever seen before. The meteor begins to shrink rather quickly. After a few weeks it is gone.

The scientists forget about it. But strange things begin to happen on the farm. The vegetables grow to huge sizes. But they taste horrible. Then they crumble to gray dust. The farm animals and the wild animals begin acting strangely. Then they, too, begin to decay.

And the farmer, Nahum Gardner, his wife and boys—what happened to them?

First, the farmer's wife begins to go mad. "When the boys grew afraid of her, and Thaddeus nearly fainted at the way she made faces at him, he decided to keep her locked in the attic. By July she had ceased to speak and crawled on all fours, and before the month was over Nahum got the mad notion that she was slightly luminous . . ."

Things just got worse and worse on the farm. When a friend came to visit, he found that the boys had disappeared. Nahum was dying or, to be more accurate, rotting. The friend went upstairs to find out about the wife who had been locked in the attic:

"When he did enter he saw something dark in the corner, and upon seeing it more clearly he screamed outright . . . the terrible thing about the horror was that it very slowly and perceptibly moved as it continued to crumble."

The cause of all these unnatural terrors is a thing. It doesn't have a body or a shape. It is just a color, but not a color that has ever been seen before on this earth. The thing was brought to earth by the meteorite. It lived in the bottom of the farmer's well. It drew its strength from the living things around it. The more they died, the stronger it became.

At the end of the story the color shoots back into space. But one person sees a small part of it fall back to earth. The whole terror may begin again.

The Colour Out of Space is a truly frightening story. Someday you may wish to read it yourself. Let me give you one piece of advice. Don't read it just before going to sleep.

Index

About the Author

DANIEL COHEN has fourteen Archway paperbacks in print, including some titles he has co-authored with his wife, Susan. Among his popular monster and ghost collections are: *Ghostly Terrors, The Greatest Monsters in the World, Horror in the Movies, The Monsters of Star Trek, Real Ghosts, Supermonsters,* and *The World's Most Famous Ghosts.*

A former managing editor of *Science Digest* magazine, Mr. Cohen has a degree in journalism from the University of Illinois. He appears frequently on radio and television and has lectured at colleges and universities throughout the country. Currently he lives with his wife, young daughter, one dog and four cats in Port Jervis, New York.